All That Is You

Alyssa Satin Capucilli
illustrated by Devon Holzwarth

Henry Holt and Company
New York

Henry Holt and Company, *Publishers since 1866*
Henry Holt® is a registered trademark of Macmillan Publishing Group, LLC
120 Broadway, New York, NY 10271 • mackids.com

Our books may be purchased in bulk for promotional, educational, or business use.
Please contact your local bookseller or the Macmillan Corporate and
Premium Sales Department at (800) 221-7945 ext. 5442 or by
email at MacmillanSpecialMarkets@macmillan.com.

Library of Congress Cataloging-in-Publication Data
Names: Capucilli, Alyssa Satin, 1957- author. | Holzwarth, Devon, illustrator.
Title: All that is you / Alyssa Satin Capucilli ; illustrated by Devon Holzwarth.
Description: First edition. | New York, NY : Henry Holt Books for
Young Readers, 2022. | Audience: Ages 2-6. | Audience: Grades K-1. |
Summary: Illustrations and rhyming text celebrate the treasured
intergenerational bonds of love and joy that connect everyone everywhere.
Identifiers: LCCN 2021046626 | ISBN 9781627797023 (hardcover)
Subjects: CYAC: Stories in rhyme. | Love–Fiction. | Belonging (Social
psychology)–Fiction. | LCGFT: Picture books. | Stories in rhyme.
Classification: LCC PZ8.3.C1935 Al 2022 | DDC [E]--dc23
LC record available at https://lccn.loc.gov/2021046626

First edition, 2022
Book design by Ashley Caswell
The art for this book was created with gouache, watercolor, colored pencil, and digital finishing.
Printed in China by Toppan Leefung Printing Ltd., Dongguan City, Guangdong Province

ISBN 978-1-62779-702-3 (hardcover)
1 3 5 7 9 10 8 6 4 2

For my family—always the wide in my world,
the home in my soon . . .
—A. S. C.

For Miranda and Griffin, and all that you are
—D. H.

You're the hop in my happy,
the SPLASH in my puddle,

the sing in my song,
the close in my cuddle.

You're the sun when rain showers,
the hush as snow falls,

the castle in my sand,
the leap when waves call.

You're my "Gather 'round the table,"
the "Make room for one more,"

the share in my together,
the warm hug at the door.

You're the magic in my beanstalk,
my sail across the sea,

the story of
my painting,

the twist and shout with me!

You're the sunflower in my garden,
the giggle in each surprise,

the wait in every wonder,
the wind when dandelions fly!

You're the make in my cake,
the hooray when candles glow,

the sparkle in my confetti,
the wish in my . . . BLOW!

You're the tender in my night,
the rise in my shine,

the listen in my unsure,
the forgive in my unkind.

You're the tall in my shadow,
the curious along my way,

the cheer in my own path,

the peace in a too-busy day.

You're the wide in my world,

the home in my soon,

the star that found my dream,
the glow of my moon.

You're the give in my love,

the boundless in it, too.

And forever

tucked inside

of me,

is all that is you.